W9-CHB-692

This book belongs to:
_____

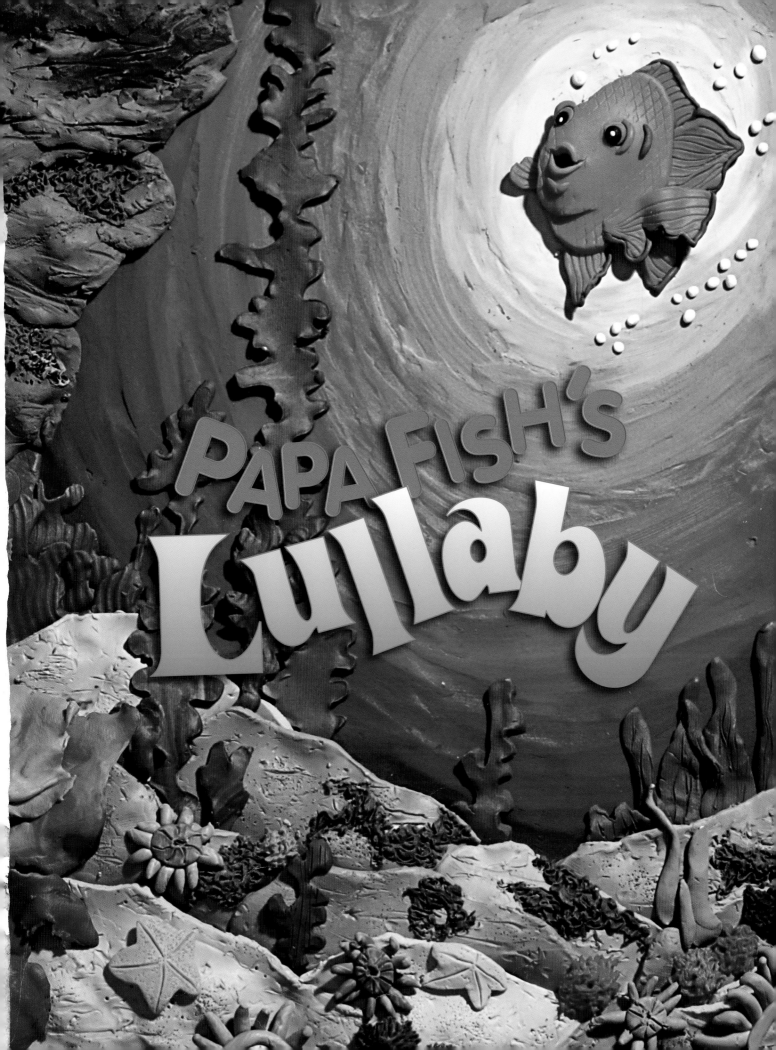

The illustrations were created using plasticine clay, photographed, and finalized in Adobe Photoshop
The text and display type were set in VAG Rounded and Curlz MT
Composed in the United States of America
Designed by Lois A. Rainwater
Edited by Kristen McCurry

NORTHWORD

Books for Young Readers
11571 K-Tel Drive
Minnetonka, MN 55343
www.tnkidsbooks.com

Library of Congress Cataloging-in-Publication Data

Hubbell, Patricia.
Papa fish's lullaby / by Patricia Hubbell ; illustrated by Susan Eaddy.
p. cm.
ISBN 978-1-55971-965-0 (hc)
1. Marine animals--Juvenile literature. I. Eaddy, Susan, ill. II. Title.

QL122.2.H83 2007

578.77--dc22   2006011609

Printed in Singapore
10 9 8 7 6 5 4 3 2 1

For Merry Iverson

—P.H.

For my mother, and in memory

of my father, who loved fish

—S.E.

Papa Fish's Lullaby

by **Patricia Hubbell**

illustrated by **Susan Eaddy**

NorthWord
Minnetonka, Minnesota

Little fish,
brave in the sea,

swish your tail, swim home to me.

In green waters, turtles rest,
floating where the white waves crest.

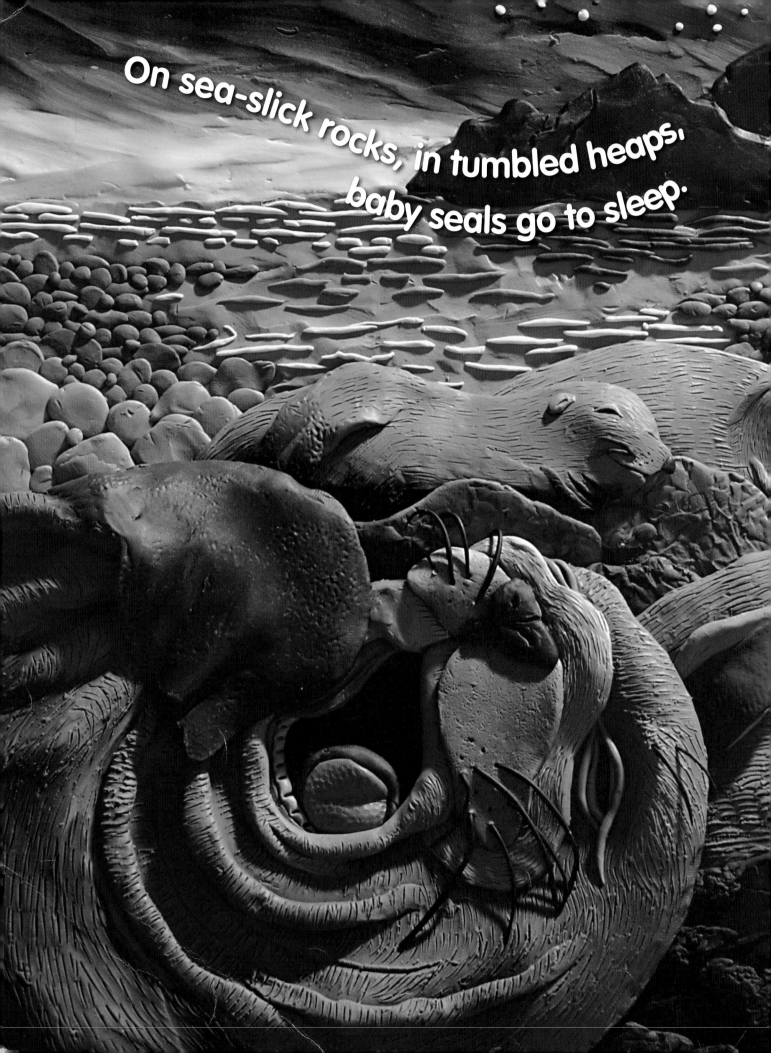

On sea-slick rocks, in tumbled heaps, baby seals go to sleep.

Where thick kelp forests swirl and sway,
seahorses cling, to end their day.

Sea otters hold their babies tight.
They watch the moon light up the night.

Dolphins take one final leap.

Beneath the stars they go to sleep.

Bobbing on a gentle swell,
seagull moms sing "All is well."

Moon jellies, drifting with the tides,

spend sleepy nights on starlit rides.

Far from harm and crashing wave, octopus rests inside his cave.

Flying low across the moon, wild geese will be sleeping soon.

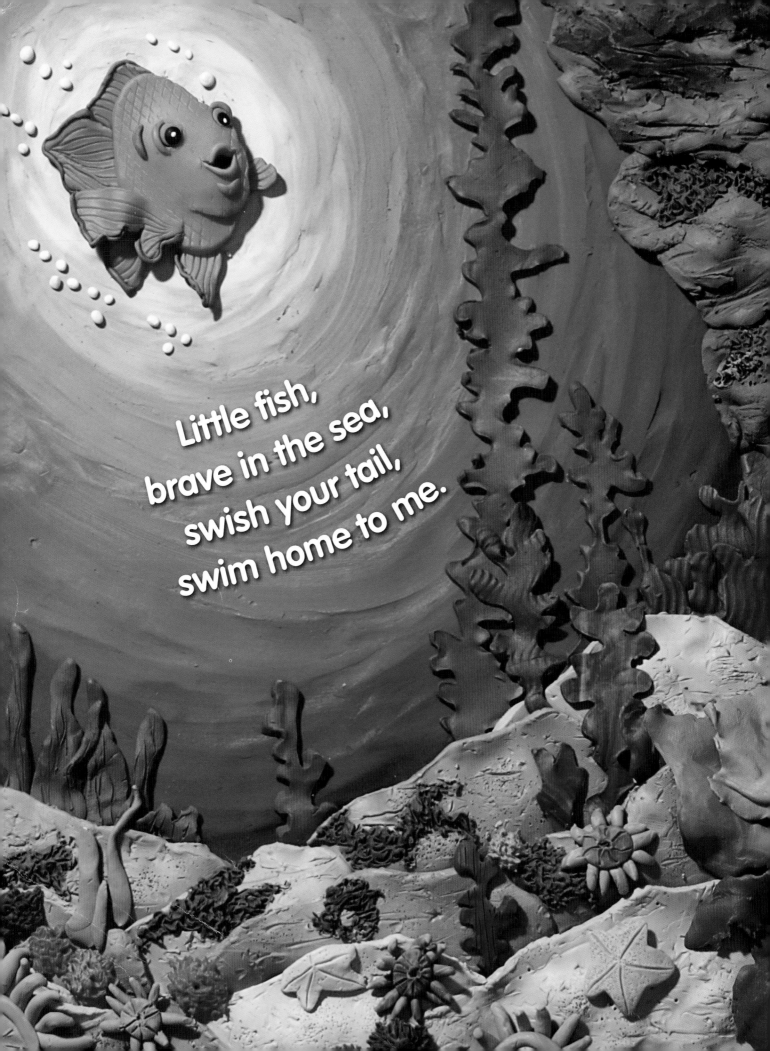

Little fish,
brave in the sea,
swish your tail,
swim home to me.

Rest, my little fish, rest.

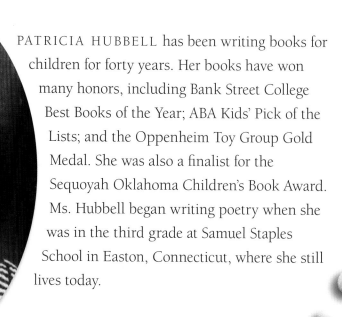

PATRICIA HUBBELL has been writing books for children for forty years. Her books have won many honors, including Bank Street College Best Books of the Year; ABA Kids' Pick of the Lists; and the Oppenheim Toy Group Gold Medal. She was also a finalist for the Sequoyah Oklahoma Children's Book Award. Ms. Hubbell began writing poetry when she was in the third grade at Samuel Staples School in Easton, Connecticut, where she still lives today.

When her Mom framed the rooster she drew in kindergarten, SUSAN EADDY decided that she wanted to be an artist. Since then she has been building on those basic skills and has never lost her love for modeling clay.

Susan was an award-winning art director for fifteen years. She has illustrated over 80 books and covers in the educational market, and her work can be found on wall borders, greeting cards, and puzzles. She lives in Nashville, Tennessee, with her art professor husband and two fat cats.

Papa Fish's Lullaby is her first picture book. You can see more of her work at www.susaneaddy.com.